For Karen, who chose Lupin from
The Wainwright Shelter, Animal Rescue Cumbria, 1990
~
J.L.

MYRIAD BOOKS LIMITED
35 Bishopsthorpe Road, London SE26 4PA

First published in 2000 by
FRANCES LINCOLN LIMITED
4 Torriano Mews, Torriano Avenue
London NW5 2RZ

ISBN 1 84746 004 6

EAN 9 781 84746 004 2

Printed in China

MISSING!

Jonathan Langley

MYRIAD BOOKS LIMITED

When Daisy went to nursery …

… Lupin stayed at home.

After nursery Lupin would meet Daisy on the corner
at the end of their road.

When the holidays started, Daisy didn't go to nursery ...

... but Lupin didn't know.

Daisy was busy all morning ...

... and so was Lupin.

Lupin went for his morning stroll

and arrived at the corner at the usual time.

Daisy hung up her painting, then looked for Lupin.
"Time for your fishy biscuits, Lupin!" she called.

Lupin waited at the corner.

'Where is Daisy?' he wondered. 'Has she gone on a school trip? Or to a birthday party? When is she coming back?'

Daisy looked in Lupin's favourite places,
but she couldn't find him anywhere.
"Where are you, Lupin?" Daisy called.

Lupin wandered along the road towards Nursery. Suddenly
Lupin raced back to the corner. 'Perhaps a big

Daisy looked everywhere. "What if a lion has

a dog leapt out of a gateway and barked at him.
dog has chased Daisy away!' he thought.

chased Lupin away! Or a shark! Oh no!" she cried.

Lupin ran to the top of the tree. He looked out as
'What if a big bird has carried Daisy

Daisy hunted for lions and sharks, but there were none to be
'Has he been turned into a frog or

ar as he could see, but there was no sign of Daisy.
off!' he thought. 'I must rescue her!'

een. 'Has Lupin been stolen by a wicked witch?' she thought.
ocked up in a tower? I must rescue him!'

'What has happened to Daisy?' Lupin thought.
'Is she lost? Is she all alone and can't find her way home?'

Daisy looked out of her window across the town.
'Is Lupin lost?' she wondered. 'Is he all alone
and can't find his way home?'

'Daisy has gone away,' thought Lupin. 'Perhaps she's

"Lupin has gone away," said Daisy. "Perhaps I didn't

gone to live somewhere else. Perhaps she's got a new cat.'

feed him enough. Perhaps he's found a new home."

'Lupin doesn't love me any more,'

…but I must do something special

thought Daisy. 'He's never coming back ...

just in case he does come back.'

Lupin went round to the back of the house. It was very

'... but perhaps she's left me a little bit

quiet. 'Daisy doesn't love me any more,' he thought ...

of food. What's that in my basket?'

"Lupin!"

"WHERE HAVE YOU BEEN?!"